THE STONES

MERSHIYA J

AF657993

BlueRose ONE
Stories Matter
NewDelhi • London

BLUEROSE PUBLISHERS
India | U.K.

For permissions requests or inquiries regarding this publication, please contact:

BLUEROSE PUBLISHERS
www.BlueRoseONE.com
info@bluerosepublishers.com
+91 8882 898 898
+4407342408967

ISBN: 978-93-6783-835-8

Cover Design: Aman Sharma
Typesetting: Pooja Sharma

First Edition: January 2025

Contents

1. The Beginning

'I am bored." said Venoma-again.

"You have repeated the same sentence for the 26th time now" Veronica replied patiently.

"How about I repeat for the 27th time?" Vespera asked, trying to cheer up her older sisters.

There you have it. Another typical day at the residence of these three siblings. The middle child, Venoma, sat in the middle of their massive room repeating a single sentence—the truth—while Veronica, the oldest sister, peacefully read a book in her chair. Vespera, the youngest, was engaged in her normal pastime of creating lifelike illustrations that, for a split second, appear to be moving.

"Dinner!" their mother's voice shouted from the kitchen. Venoma ran out of the room, most likely to see who reaches the ground floor of their house first. Vespera took the challenge and charged through the door. Their elder sister closed the book and came walking down.

"What about you?" Veronica asked her mother, who left the kitchen and went straight to her office area.

"In a minute or two." However, their mother never left the room even after the three girls had finished eating and gone to bed. Vespera stated that she would only go to bed after completing her artwork. Venoma hardly gave a word. She headed straight for their enormous, three-person bed that sits in the corner of their room. After Veronica promised to wait for her younger sister, she went to the desk and sat in her favorite chair.

Greetings from the lives of these siblings. After completing their final exams with flawless scores, all three of them are now extremely bored. However, none of them are aware of the shocking twist that completely alters the plot.

"Shall I switch off the lights?" Vespera asked.

"Yes please." Her sister replied. Venoma was already fast asleep. The other two sisters settled onto the limited space they each had.

"Good night Vespera."

"Same to you sis."

"Guys." -that was Venoma's voice.

"You are still awake? Wait, what is that?"-this was Vespera's.

"What is what?" Veronica understood after turning to face the room instead of the wall. From the middle of their room... there was something. It was pretty much illuminating the whole place. Three different colors of light- *red, blue and white.*

"What is that..." Venoma went a little closer.

"Don't touch it!" Veronica warned her, but she did anyway. The lighting effect stopped. The youngest sister smartly turned on the light immediately. A box. A very, very bizarre box, well it looks like one. It was sitting in the middle of their room.

"Where did it come from?" Vespera asked, but the other two were very interested in a question that kept on repeating in their mind.

"What is this thing?" Both said at once.

"Well, we cannot answer that without opening this...box" Venoma said without giving up her curiosity.

"Do not open it!" the oldest sibling proved she is the most protective in their group

"That thing... it looks... very ancient...I wonder what it is made of?" Vespera mirrored the second oldest sister's personality.

"What should we do now?" Veronica questioned, not her sisters, but herself but before she could think of an answer,

"There is only one thing we can do right now." After telling her siblings, Venoma opened the box without saying anything else.

"What the heck?! Venoma! Why would you act in such way?" Their older sister dashed forward to shut the box close, but she had to shield her eyes from the glaring light that was now gradually getting brighter as well.

"What's happening?" Vespera screamed. When the other two turned around, they saw their sister's body disintegrating into minuscule fragments and vanishing within the box. "No! Vespe..." Venoma broke off midsentence. Like her younger sister, she too was doomed to an uncertain future. Veronica was clueless about what to do. It's obvious that no one gave her advice on what to do when her two younger sisters are fading away. She felt incredibly light suddenly, like she was raised into the air. Glancing down, she saw that her hands were vanishing into the odd box, the main cause of everything. Slowly, she too disappeared into the darkness.

2. The New World

"I hope you are happy now, aren't you? Finally, you got rid of your boredom!" Veronica shouted.

"You are talking like as though I wanted all this! Like I wanted for the three of us to be stuck in a nightmarish realm or whatever this place is, would I really wish for that?" Venoma shouted back at her sister.

"Then who on earth asked to open that stupid box?!"

"I never expected such a result! I would've done nothing if I knew this is where we would find ourselves at just because I opened that cursed object!"

"Cursed object?" Vespera interrupted the quarrel between her elder sisters. After being sucked into the box, all three of them fell through, most likely a portal or something, and eventually reached the solid ground. They looked up to find a place which had no sign of humanity. There was... nothing. Plain emptiness. The ground itself was a mixture of brown and black. No greenery at all. The only thing which they could see in the empty world was a black door. A very enormous door with a statue of two red colored dragons on either side. The door seems to lead nowhere. There was nothing behind the door. Again, just plain, empty land. The other directions seem to have no end. There was obviously no exit to go back to their home.

"Stop shouting, can you?" Vespera said after she had enough of all the screaming and blaming.

"Think about what we should do now..." She said while making her short hair even messier than it is already.

"For God's sake Vespera please don't do that!" Veronica said that, but her mind suddenly diverted to the fate of her own long hair at the movement.

"Nonsense! This is not the time to think about it!" She said to herself. "First we should get out of here! And then you can worry about all the useless things."

"Glad I am not like you both." Venoma said with no worries about her appearance. Her straight hair always fell back onto its place above her shoulder.

"Alright we were talking about what we should do in this current situation." Veronica said deeply thinking about the answer to her own question.

"I have an idea!" Venoma answered her sister's inquiry almost immediately.

"You better not speak right now, on second thought, don't even open your mouth!" the oldest sister yelled at

Venoma. They definitely don't need one of her ideas again.

"I say we enter the black door in front of us." Vespera said suddenly.

"You... are not serious right?" The last thing Veronica wants is to go check what is inside that door. She was afraid Venoma would bring that thought into consideration, instead of what Vespera had.

"Hey! It would've been me who said that first if she hadn't stopped me!" the second youngest sister protested.

"My name is Veronica!" the oldest sister likes to be called more by her name instead of pronouns.

"We get it! Your name is not the most important thing in the world alright!" it was Vespera who shouted this time. They are stuck in a whole other world and all her dear sisters care about is their name.

"Ok, I've had enough of this what-should-we-do fight." Venoma said not being able to stay in a single place for too long after noticing the once-in-a-lifetime opportunities in front of them.

"The highest voting goes for opening the door and entering to see whatever lies behind it. So, Veronica, we are going inside whether you accept it or not. You can either come with us or sit right here and keep thinking about something that is impossible." Venoma challenged her elder sister.

"What is impossible exactly?" Veronica questioned.

"Escaping from this place with some shortcuts you have made up in your mind right now." That is the truth. They have no choice but to face the challenges that they would find inside that door.

"Fine"

"Fine what?" Vespera asked who was quietly listening to her older sisters speak for a long time.

"I would... come with you guys... inside... that door." Veronica accepted reluctantly.

"YES! I am so proud of you sis!" Venoma jumped with excitement.

"But you both should be very careful and listen to my instructions if I really mean it." That was the only thing the oldest sister ever wanted.

"So shall we find out what's inside this mysterious door?" Vespera asked, affected by the radiating excitement from Venoma.

"We shall!" Both the older sisters accepted and pushed the door open.

3. Mythical Creatures

"I do not like this" Venoma murmured.

"Why is it so silent?" Veronica said, removing all the thoughts in her mind about what might happen next.

"What's wrong with silence?" the youngest sister asked after a while.

"Oh, you won't understand." Venoma said darkly.

"Then explain in a way I would understand." Vespera answered as usual, giving you no room for disagreement.

"Fine the problem with silence at this situation is that whenever the place is too calm, there will be something lurking in the corners waiting for the perfect time to attack." the oldest sister explained 'in a way Vespara would understand'.

"Exactly. That is why I don't like this." Venoma was sure she saw something or perhaps a shadow moves behind them.

"You also feel the same? Like as though something is moving behind us and watching every step we take?" Veronica asked one of her sisters who looked back suspiciously and turned front again to face the path on which they were walking.

"Now that you mentioned it, it feels more obvious." the middle child told with a look on her face which clearly read 'for once in your life, hold your mouth and don't make this any more real'.

"Where is the exit?" They all realized they were travelling down a path that seemed to go on forever when Vespera inquired abruptly. After entering through the door, it immediately closed. Their pathway was lit by burning torches made of fire which were on the sides of the only road they could take. That was all they could see since darkness was spreading everywhere except for the path they faced in front of them.

"All right, to be honest, I'm afraid now. Will we be on foot forever?" After they had been strolling for a while, Venoma accepted.

"I am afraid that might be the truth here." The youngest child, after they had been lost in the dark for a while, finally accepted.

"No, I don't think..." Veronica stopped before she finished the sentence. The other two also stopped. They slowly turned around and... blazing fire came rushing in front of their face. They ducked immediately screaming. The fire lit up the whole place, which ended up being a room with the walls and the ceiling in emerald green and the floor was blood red.

And the cause of the sudden attack was... a dragon. Its body seemed to be made of fire itself. Its wings were folded probably because the room won't fit. It attacked again and this time the target seemed to be Venoma. All three of them ran in different directions and the dragon followed Venoma, continuously attacking her using the fire coming from its mouth. At one point, the dragon cornered Venoma with no escape.

“Venoma!” the other two sisters exclaimed but, a... shadow emerged behind Venoma as the dragon was about to slay its first victim with its charged assault. In the speed of light, the second youngest sister was reunited with her sisters by the shadow, who was thankfully a human.

“Who are you?" Venoma questioned her rescuer.

"Questions afterwards, we should first get to safety now." it was a male voice. He was wearing a hood covering his face and seemed pretty calm for the current situation. The dragon seemed to be more interested in the new guy. It charged one more of its powerful attacks on him. But unexpectedly, he pulled Veronica as a shield to protect himself along with the other two sisters.

"What hell are you doing?! Veronica!" the youngest sister screamed but...

Nothing happened. The dragon didn't attack. It stopped right there doing nothing.

"That's right. Know your place." The boy said while carefully making sure that Veronica is the only person the dragon is facing. He quickly pulled Vespera into the shade too.

"I don't understand. Why did it stop? Why isn't the dragon attacking?" the eldest sister asked confused.

"Do you want it attack?" the boy asked with a laughing tone in his voice.

"Of course I don't!" Veronica said quickly. *Who is this boy?* she thought to herself. They reached the pathway in which they were walking for so long and... the dragon didn't even move. Venoma thought for sure they would never reach the exit, but the boy took a torch a showed to the dark path which no longer had been lit and there was a door. The exit. It was right there, and the mysterious boy pushed it open a little. He told Vespera to go first and then pushed Venoma out too. The oldest sister found herself standing along with her siblings in an instant after the door was closed.

"Now, who are you?" Vespera asked the question which her other two sisters were also dying to ask.

"Ok, so first, my name is Oliver." the boy- Oliver said and lifted the hood covering his face. He had blue eyes just like Venoma, but Her's is more darker. His hair resembled Vespera's, short and messy.

"So? Finally got the answer to your question?" He asked after he had enough of the staring.

"Yeah... well, I am Veronica, she is the middle child, Venoma, and she is the youngest, Vespera." the oldest child introduced herself and her siblings.

"Good to know." Oliver replied smiling.

"Where did you come from?" the youngest sister asked curiously.

"Well, I got stuck inside that room with the dragon long before you three..." He said thoughtfully.

"How long?"

"About 2 years."

"2 years?!" all three of the sisters were not sure if they heard him properly. This boy stayed inside that dark room without food or water for 2 whole years, along with a dragon which won't thick twice before having him as dinner or burning him to ash the second it meets him.

"Don't be that surprised! You'll understand when the time comes." He assured them. And somehow all three of the sisters managed to hold their questions back.

"So, what now?" Vespera asked looking around. They came back to the place they had started. The empty land. The only difference is that the ground is now a mixture of assorted colors in which all were a type of blue. The other new improvement is that there was a new door waiting for them, it was in blue color with a statue on either side of it that looked like it was made to resemble the waves made in the oceans.

"You ready?" Oliver asked when he noticed his new friends facing the new challenge waiting for them.

"Yes." the three of them said at once. Unlike the first time, there were four of them now.

4. Who are you?

"Why? Why is it always so silent?" Venoma asked looking around.

"I think it is better. You don't want something to attack you the second you step in, or do you?" Oliver asked, also looking around. They expected much more than what they were currently seeing. At least darkness. But this time after the door was opened, flashing light blinded their eyes.

It was really tranquil. The sun was beaming, yet it didn't appear like there was a sky. Very pure water filled the ground, yet it only rose to the level of their toes. With nothing else around and just silence to deal with, it nearly looked like the epitome of an introvert's fantasy. They are aware, however, that something is waiting for them.

"So let me guess, we need to walk another mile or two and then wait for something to show itself and then we should run around..." Veronica predicted what would be happening in a minute.

"Well, I am not sure who would *wait* for something to attack, I am not stopping you from." Oliver said looking at his reflection in the water and making his hair even messier just like Vespera.

"At this point, I am not sure if I have control over my legs anymore." The middle child complained after a long time. Her other sisters also had to accept, maybe even Oliver would say the same.

"Oh God, how much longer?" Veronica also finally broke. She has never in life kept walking for this long.

"What is that... we finally reached the end!" the youngest sister said suddenly. Clearly, they have. A new door was right in front of them.

"Don't move!" Oliver yelled. They came to an instant stop. It was there. Their new foe. The groundwater was gradually rising to the surface and taking on the form of a monster.

"What is... is that a Pegasus?" Veronica inquired after the water finished making its masterpiece.

"Seriously? The horse from the Greek mythology?" the youngest child asked not believing her eyes.

"The *winged* horse from Greek mythology." Oliver corrected her. The sacred creature opened its eyes which were in the beautiful dark blue color, surprisingly the same color as Venoma's eyes. But as beautiful as it was, it was powerful. The main target seemed to Veronica. The water on the ground raised to form a huge tidal wave. All four of them ran in different directions-again. The creature spread its wings and went straight for Veronica.

"Venoma!" Oliver shouted. "Protect your older sister!" Without thinking, the second eldest sister jumped in front of the white Pegasus and...

It stopped. Right there without attacking. Vespera thought both her sisters were dead for sure but no. Nothing happened. Oliver quickly came in front of Venoma and looked at the mythical horse straight to the eyes. It... backed down.

"Venoma take your older sister to the exit." Oliver said or most likely commanded, but the middle sister obeyed anyway. Oliver followed the other two siblings to the exit and the horse did not even move. They opened the door and went out to reach another new empty world. Venoma, the last to leave, looked at the sacred horse which disappeared back into the water.

"Alright now honestly answer my question, who are you? Why did that... Pegasus stop its attack after seeing Venoma? And the same with the dragon. And... why did the horse completely leave us alone when it saw you?" Veronica asked the questions in place of her other two sisters.

"I told my name is Oliver. And as for the other questions, you'll understand when the time comes. Now we should think about entering next door to face new challenges..." Oliver said walking forward and looking around. This time they were standing in a colorless world. Everywhere they faced just emptiness (no surprise there) and... the color gray. Nothing else. The new entrance was also gray. The statues resembled a cyclone this time.

"You won't say anything more than that?" Vespera questioned Oliver.

"No" He replied simply.

"Fine, don't." Venoma sighed.

"Come on, cheer up." Oliver said after looking at his friend's faces. "Ready to face whatever lies inside?" He asked, bringing a hint of smile.

"Come on." Veronica said, running ahead. The four of them pushed open the gray door.

5. Sylph –The Mythological Creatures

"This is completely unexpected." Venoma said or most likely shouted.

"I accept with you sis." the eldest sister said covering her eyes. On entering the last two realms of doom, it was so silent, and the second one was so peaceful. And yet, immediately after closing the door behind them, all four of them were hit by the most powerful winds they ever faced. Vespera was almost lifted onto the air but thankfully Oliver saved her, not to mention the fact that he was laughing the whole time (Vespera had not yet forgiven him for that.)

"We should be careful." Oliver warned them. "I am sure some or the other type of mythical creatures will be hiding where we least expect."

"Really? You are worried about the mythical creatures I see. Well, I am worried that we will not be able to cross this obstacle without entering that swirling tornado over there!" Vespera exclaimed.

"What tornado?" Oliver asked since his eyes are a complete blur because of all the dust and mist.

"That." Vespera said pointing towards a direction. Sure enough, it was extremely huge.

"There is no way we can cross that without dying in the process." the oldest sister said looking at it.

"It is suicide." Venoma gave up.

"I thought... it would be a perfect challenge for us..." Oliver said looking down.

"You are kidding right?" Vespera could not believe it. A challenge? Venoma was right, the actual name for this so-called challenge is 'suicide'.

"But we cannot sit here doing nothing." Oliver protested.

"He is right." Venoma said after a long time. "The sooner we get out of here, the better."

"But you do realize that before getting out, we'll be long dead?" Veronica said, siding with her youngest sister.

"Exactly." Vespera accepted.

"Fine. Sit right here. Come on Venoma, we need to cross these obstacles, we got so much work to do..." Oliver suddenly walked ahead facing the wind. Venoma understood his plan.

"You are right Oliver." She played along and went after her friend. Oliver looked behind and managed to hold his laughter after seeing the horrified looks on Vespera's and her oldest sister's faces.

"Alright!" Veronica gave up and pulled her younger sister to catch up with the others. Oliver, meanwhile, was trying extremely hard not to laugh. He looked at Venoma who was trying the same.

"Ok, now are you guys ready?" Venoma asked them after getting close to the dangerous cyclone.

"No!" Vespera shouted. Oliver rolled his eyes. His friends have a huge amount of courage.

"The two of you should follow me and Vespera." Oliver confused them with his words.

"Why me?" the youngest sister questioned.

"Because you are the only one here who can lead the way."

"Why is that?"

"Your eyes can see the path more clearly than ours."

"Is that because I told you there was a tornado in the middle of nowhere?"

"That's because you are the only one who can see the tornado."

"And why is that?"

"You are asking me? Whose eyes are those?"

"Fine I'll lead the way. I need someone beside me at least."

"Where are your sisters going to go? No one is asking you to walk alone into darkness." With that the conversation or the argument has ended. Walking straight into a cyclone is more terrifying than it sounds. Much. More. Terrifying. You do not even know if you are walking on the ground or in the air. Except Vespera, they do not even know where they are placing their foot.

"Oh God save me." Venoma prayed after her vision got completely dark because of the dust entering her eyes.

"Can you really see nothing?" Vespera shouted so that her friend and sisters could hear her.

"Why what's wrong?" Oliver asked, rubbing his eyes to see something at least.

"I think we are in danger." the youngest child shouted again.

"What on earth is that?" Venoma asked after her eyes adjusted.

"What are you talking about... " Oliver started but soon saw what his friends were talking about. They were in the middle of the swirling wind and... there was something, no way to define it.

"A Sylph." Oliver said to himself, but Venoma heard it anyway.

"What's a Sylph?" She asked but the one who gave her the answer was one of her siblings.

"It is a supernatural air spirit that is immortal but has no soul. It came from the Greek mythology." Vespera recited it like a poem.

"Where did you learn that from?" Veronica asked her youngest sister.

"I don't know." That was Vespera's answer.

"We should get out of here immediately." Oliver made a quick decision. His friends followed it. But then something unexpected happened. The wind cleared itself and formed a dome-like structure around the Sylph and the four of them.

"What's happening?" Veronica asked, obviously scared like any other human being. Oliver understood.

"We need your permission to pass this wind realm safely." When he spoke to the sylph that was floating in midair, it opened its eyes. They matched its hair color, being black. The Sylph's most admirable characteristic is that its wings are made of feathers like those of an angel but resemble the devil's wings.

"I am curious to know if you would accept." Oliver continued. "We would be honored if you could help us go back to our home and leave this place. I assure you; we won't disturb you again."

"My name is Celia." The Sylph- Celia said with what we can say the most beautiful voice ever.

"Well Celia, would you allow us to pass your realm safely?" Oliver questioned.

"I introduced myself, why won't you too?" Celia requested all four of them.

"My name is Oliver."

"My name's Veronica."

"Mine is Venoma."

"My name is Vespera."

"Such beautiful names." Celia appreciated it. "But why is your name 'Venoma'? You do realize that it means 'poison'."

"It was my mother who picked it. I also like it since it is incredibly unique." the middle sister answered.

"Oliver means 'hope', Veronica means 'victory', Vespera means 'evening star'..." Celia said to herself.

"Celia, all of us would be honored if you could let us pass..." Oliver tried again.

"Yes, you already told me that a few hundred times." The Sylph cut him off. "But if you want me to let you go, give a valuable reason or defeat me to leave." Three of them couldn't believe what they heard. How are they supposed to fight a supernatural being and defeat it? Oliver thought of a valuable reason, but he knew Celia would decline it. Meanwhile the second oldest sister thought of a plan.

"We would like to go home, that's our reason." She said without care. Oliver gasped. *Is her brain completely dead or something? Now surely the Sylph would kill us all.* He thought. Celia laughed.

"That is your answer? Sorry Venoma, now we will see your fighting skills..." The Sylph landed on the ground.

"Nobody is going to show their fighting skills Celia, I just defeated you." Venoma replied to the invitation.

"Defeated me how?" Celia asked confused.

"You didn't tell in what way we should defeat you..." Oliver realized.

"So, I made a challenge that if you didn't accept whatever reason we give, you lose." Venoma explained. *She is smarter than I thought.* Oliver said to himself.

"But that is so absurd, if I accept the reason, you give me, that also means I should let you out of here according to the deal." The Sylph protested.

"Exactly." Venoma gave her a definitive answer.

Celia laughed. "You live up to your name Venoma." She said and the cyclone disappeared. A new exit emerged in front of them. On leaving, Venoma looked behind to see the Sylph telling the last words to her-

"The future of Vigos is in your hands."

6. The Unexpected Battle

"Ok I think my legs have departed." Venoma said after long, engrossing hours of walking.

"Don't be stupid. They are still there." Oliver said looking ahead.

"How on earth are you able to stand upright? I mean, I'm not sure I get it. You seem so energized, yet the three of us are falling apart after walking for around two hours." Veronica complained once more.

"If you all are done talking, I would like to say something." The youngest sister interrupted them.

"What is it?" Oliver enquired. They noticed a hill after leaving the Sylph Celia, indicating that they will have to climb it to reach the other side. When Venoma realized it, she nearly passed out, but Oliver was able to cheer her up. They had been at the highest point for a while when Vespera noticed something.

"What is what?" Oliver asked confused.

"Oliver, you know what? I have never met someone with worse eyesight than you. Or perhaps it is your observing skills which need improvement." Vespera shook her head in disappointment as she said.

"Hey!" Oliver protests but deep down he knows that is the truth.

"I accept with my sister." Veronica also supported the opinion.

"I am against it alright." Venoma said, no, she shouted "I cannot see anything that Vespera thought was interesting... " only then she realized. Following the direction of Venoma's eyes, Oliver also saw what his friends are talking about.

"That looks like... " Vespera tried to describe it.

"A castle." the eldest sister found the right word.

"Not just any castle. It was once made of white marble but now of black obsidian. The symbol of good now is the proof that tells us evil still exists." Oliver said while slipping into a new world inside his mind.

"How do you know all this?" Veronica asked, bringing her friend back to the present in the process.

"I just know it." Oliver gave an incomplete answer half-heartedly. The oldest sibling sighed. They would never get a valuable answer from Oliver. They thought going downhill would be easy, but it isn't! Venoma gave up halfway in the verge of tears, but Oliver somehow (again) managed to cheer her up. Vespera also was about to break down, but the castle was just out of reach. Finally, they reached the gigantic gates.

"I don't think so any human will be able to push and open those gates." Veronica was convinced.

"We'll see about that." Oliver and Venoma both accepted the challenge. Both the oldest and youngest sibling relaxed for the first time after hours. Meanwhile, the other two members of the group summoned all their energy and might. Finally, Venoma and her friend were finally able to open the massive castle's gates on their third attempt.

"I... never thought it would be so beautiful..." Venoma accepted. It was beautiful. But maybe Vespera would also be fascinated as much as her sister if the only color visible wasn't black. Veronica was not admiring the castle either.

"So, what should we do now?" she asked.

"We should explore more and move around rather than staying at a single place. Perhaps we will find something." Oliver said while already walking forward. Eventually he was followed by his other three friends.

"Oliver." Venoma spoke after a long time. The other two are far behind, checking every room they pass through.

"What happened?" Oliver asked absent-mindedly.

"Vigos."

Oliver gasped, that one word got Venoma his full attention.

"So, you do know about it." Venoma said. "Can you explain what it means?"

"Where did you learn that word?" Oliver asked horrified.

"The Sylph mentioned it just before I closed the door. 'The future of Vigos is in your hands.' Those were her exact words." Venoma answered. She was about to repeat her question again, but Oliver gave the answer anyways.

"Vigos is something you won't understand." he walked forward without another word.

"Then explain in a way I would understand!" Venoma ran after him. But she knows he will never give the actual answer they need. It wasn't long before the others caught up with them. Venoma didn't say anything else, which was fine with Oliver. They entered the castle's throne room, only to find that there was only one throne.

"You won't say the reason even if you know it." Veronica told the truth when her younger sister asked why there is only one majestic, black throne sitting in front of them.

"Forget about it! What is that in the first place?" Venoma asked, pointing to the side of the throne.

"What is... oh." Oliver noticed something important faster for the first time.

"That thing..." Vespera started.

"Appeared in our room at the very start." the oldest sister ended the sentence. It was the cause of all these problems they were facing now. The box. It was sitting so innocently right in front of them.

"Watch out!" Oliver gave a startled scream. He sent the four of them flying into the earth. The sword was aimed directly at their heads and none of them saw it coming.

"You dodged it? Well, after a long wait, a worthy opponent at last!" Suddenly, a new voice said out of nowhere. Glancing up, all four of them saw their foe. He was positioned at the entrance. One hand holding a yellow sword, the other challenging them to fight.

"Veronica listen to me carefully." Oliver's tone changed to a serious mood. "No matter what happens, do not stop! Get to the box which is currently illuminating the whole place! That is the way out of this nightmare! Take your sisters too." They were running in circles around the room, barely managing to dodge the attacks.

"But what about you?" Venoma asked the first thing she thought of.

"Don't worry about me." Her friend assured them and ran in a different direction. Their enemy, who they were not sure, was a human, seemed to target Oliver.

"Come on!" Veronica pulled her siblings and followed her friend's instructions but...

"Oh, I can see your plan alright." Their opponent said and to stop them from getting close to the box, the room extended so long that the end wasn't even visible.

"Don't stop!" Oliver shouted after almost dying from one attack. "This is more of an illusion! Your goal is much closer than you think!"

"You are smarter than many I've seen. What's your name?" The enemy asked.

"Oliver."

"I see... are you aware that your name means 'hope'? Fitting you, isn't it? Mine is Dynamo. The translation is generator of *electricity*."

Oliver froze after hearing those words. At that point, his rival revealed his winning card. With his free hand, he captured the air, and a yellowish light filled the room. Terrified, the three siblings looked back, who had been so close to the enigmatic box. A small yellow colored stone resembling a jewel appeared out of nowhere. As Oliver watched in horror, his opponent advanced in the speed of light and... *stabbed him in the heart.* Veronica and Vespera both let out screams. Venoma called out to her friend. Dynamo chuckled. He looked around at his three siblings.

7. Oliver.... Quinn

"Go to your room now."

"As you wish Mrs. Quinn." Oliver answered and followed his mother's instructions. He changed his mind as soon as he got to the entrance and slipped out through the window, using his shortcut. Even though his home was enormous, he always felt trapped by the walls. His parents barely acknowledged where he was. Even if he was dying somewhere—which he was right now—they wouldn't even care about it. It's funny how all your memories resurface in your final moments.

"It is so peaceful, but too quiet." Oliver thought to himself. He likes to spend his time on the meadow by his house, which has lovely pink blossoms. It gets too dark to stay outside by dinnertime. Before long, midnight had arrived. Oliver stood up and started to head home. When he got to his room, he climbed onto his bed. Now that the school year is over, he can sleep peacefully. Everything was normal as always, but that was before he woke up to find something illuminating his room. The box. The main reason to everything. Opening it was the biggest mistake of his life.

"Where am I?" The same empty land in front of him, with a massive door. He had no choice except to open the door and step inside the terrifying world, which he did anyways. Oliver realized right away that he would have to fight a dragon in order to get away. He's not really that bold. He has an incredible ability to stay alive despite eating anything at all.

"What should I do now?" He thought. It wasn't long before he realized that he was surrounded by walls in which... there were a lot of cravings. Oliver took one of the torch lights in the pathway and held it up to the wall to read the writings. It took time for him to understand but somehow it was easy for him. The final story was...

Vigos, the land of elements. This name was kept as the great rulers of this world, excluding the king & people – were the masters of elements. Fire, water, wind, more and more. They all lived in harmony except for the master of darkness. He wanted to rule them all. Hungry for power, he killed the others and became the one supreme leader. Vigos transformed into the type of world he would prefer. Some even joined him in fear they would lose their life. But the other elemental masters had their own plans. On dying, their abilities were passed onto the unknown ones they chose. The new elemental masters will be called to Vigos at the appropriate time. Most of them might fall against the prince of darkness but the most superior ones, fire, water, and wind will not. They will enter together and will also get guidance to bring Vigos back to life.

The only line which got Oliver's attention the most was 'They will enter together.'

"I am not the master of fire, water or wind." He said to himself. This also means he would have to wait until the three cursed ones show themselves. There were many cravings besides the introduction of the sacred land. One of them said that...

The earlier lords of elements have stationed their most trustworthy mythological creatures to watch Vigos' entry, to ensure that the ones they chose are the proper ones.

That got Oliver thinking. The dragon. It is most likely to be the mythical creature belonging to the master of fire. One of the three who shows up to Vigos might be able to control the dragon. The other two will also be able to manipulate the mythical creatures in the other realms. He would have to observe the dragon when these three will face it.

He read many other cravings but some of them seem to be destroyed, or the language wasn't understandable. At one point, the ruler of darkness's name was written but it was scribbled as though the message they were trying to convey was that no one would dare tell his name.

Oliver gave up. When hope completely seemed to be lost, the entrance opened.

Three siblings. Oliver could immediately tell they were the ones the prophecy spoke of. He followed them and after a long walk the dragon appeared. Oliver remained hidden and observed patiently. The dragon chased one of the girls, so she must not be the master of fire. So, it must be the other two. And one of them, on seeing her eyes, Oliver just, knew it. It was Veronica, her red eyes seemed to shout to Oliver that she is the one and only chosen one to manipulate fire. He managed to get out of there along with the three siblings, who do not know their true potential. The cravings gave one more crucial line...

The chosen ones will know nothing about their true powers until they touch the power stones. The master of darkness has them ever since he killed the other masters of elements. Getting close to even one of these power stones is not easy.

Oliver decided not to tell the truth about the actual place they are currently standing in. The writings also mentioned that these new elemental masters will have guidance. Maybe it was him. No, it is definitely him. They came all the way to entering Vigos.

"If only it would continue to be this easy." Oliver thought as they went inside the gates of the huge black castle.

8. Unknown Memories

"Oliver!" Venoma called out to her friend. Laughing, Dynamo drew the sword out. Oliver fell to the ground. *He is dead.* Although it is hard to accept, and no one wants to believe it... that is the reality.

"So, let's see how long you three will manage to stay alive." Dynamo mocked. But it came to an end when Venoma did the most unexpected thing possible.

She reached for the box and opened it.

"Wait... NO!" Dynamo screamed. It was the least he could do. The other two followed their sister in a fraction of seconds. Their mind was filled with many possibilities that can happen when the box is opened but,

All three of the siblings... they could not move. In their mind... memories that are not even theirs, the first memory was about a prosperous land with people cheering for a group of, well they assumed it was a group of humans who were hovering in the air. The second memory was the most interesting...

The group of supernatural people from the first memory were sitting in a room. One of the rooms in the black castle. But

the huge castle was in the color of pure white… just like Oliver mentioned.

"We got to do something." One of them said. He... well, he was unfamiliar but resembled Oliver in some way. "The prince of darkness is too powerful. None of us could stop him. Hope is completely lost."

"He is right." A guy with red eyes replied. This one looked exactly like Veronica. "We cannot stop him at this point. That's why I made a plan."

"What plan?" One of them asked. He was unfamiliar no matter in what way you look at him.

"We entrust our powers to the next generation." The one looking like Veronica said without flinching a bit. But the others gasped in a mode of unparallel shock.

"You have to accept that we have no other way. But I am listening if any of you have a perfect plan."

"But this is absurd Blaze." One of them protested. This one resembled Vespera. "First of, how would you know you are choosing the right one to give all your powers? He could be evil and end up joining the enemy."

"I already chose someone." Blaze replied. "Even Adrian agrees with me. That's why we chose three siblings. My power will go to the eldest when I die. Adrian's power, water manipulation, will go to the middle child. We were hoping

the youngest could get the power of wind, but you should agree with that, Hayate."

"Water manipulation and the power of wind?" Venoma asked from a corner. In the memory, these supernatural humans were not able to hear her.

"Fine." Hayate accepted. "But this better work out Blaze."

"Hold on, there are a lot of flaws in this plan too." An unfamiliar one interrupted.

"What is it, Eirwen?" Blaze asked without any enthusiasm.

"What if these three siblings unlocked their powers in the human realm? It could cause a huge amount of destruction. And if you die, the powers will transform into a sacred gemstone as per the rule. It won't go look for the three boys whoever you chose."

"Three girls. Veronica, Venoma and Vespera." Blaze corrected him. From the corner, the chosen siblings were looking at these guys horrified. Who are they? Clearly, they are not humans.

"What you are saying is correct, I guess. That's why I already gave a small amount of my powers to one of the girls. Adrian also did the same. You all should make a decision quickly." Blaze said to all of them.

"How will these three girls arrive at Vigos?" Eirwen questioned.

"When they are ready. With Hayate's power, manipulation of wind, Arian's power and mine, we will be able to create an instrument which controls the barrier between the human realm and Vigos, the land of elements."

"So that is what Vigos means. It is this place. This world." Venoma realized. Oliver must have known all this.

"But I am still worried about what Hayate said. What if they are evil? Or worse, what if the instrument reaches the wrong one who doesn't even have any power?" Another unfamiliar one said.

"No problem Chronos. Our mythical creatures, the dragon, Pegasus and the Sylph can take care of that. They will kill any trespassers." Blaze planned everything perfectly.

"Ok, the three powers of fire, water and wind will survive but what about ours?" Eirwen asked. The answer was simple.

"You will also do the same. Choosing a human can consume a lot of time so Adrian said that he saw the perfect ones for the job." Blaze looked at the Master of Water, Adrian, but that was when the three siblings realized he looked exactly like Venoma.

"If you accept to this idea, we can immediately go to the human realm." Adrian spoke for the first time.

"And when will our successors come to Vigos?"

" When the time comes." Blaze answered for the last time. The second memory ends. The last scene was...

Blaze, Eirwen, Chronos and the others who were sitting in the room were dead. Adrian was fighting a dark figure and seemed to be losing. He was already at the verge of death. Eventually the dark figure won. That figure, it looked at the three siblings. The face was not clear, but the eyes were, one was deep red and the other was pitch black. He raised his hands... darkness and shadows came rushing to it. In the memory, Veronica looked back, followed by her sisters. It was the white castle but... shadows were climbing on it, slowly the huge, majestic castle was completely in the color of black. The enemy laughed and disappeared into emptiness.

9. True Potential

Back to the present. Time seemed to have stopped when the three siblings were wandering through the past. The reality came crashing back. Oliver's death. The chosen ones became extremely enraged at the mere thought. The three sacred stones were still being caught by them. The key to their true potential. Dynamo was preparing for his attack.

"I'll kill you for sure!" With a cry, he charged forward. Meanwhile the three of his enemies looked up and opened their eyes. It was no longer the same. Vespera's was in a strange color of nothing but white. Everywhere Venoma looked, it was illuminated with the blue light from her eyes. It was the same with her sister Veronica, but it was red.

Dynamo's power helped him reach the end of the long hallway fast enough. He was convinced he is about to win but...

"You deserve death." The eldest sister said in a voice that did sound like Her's. She stretched her hands and closed her fists.

Dynamo *burned*, screaming. Veronica is the manipulator of fire after all. Soon the

The generator of electricity was... dead, but something was still left over for the siblings to finish.

"Let's finish this." Venoma said confidently. At least her personality didn't change. The three new masters of elements grabbed each other's hands. A powerful beam of light, red, blue and white lit up the whole... world. They were suddenly standing in a new place, or we should say hovering in the air. The dry ground seemed to get a new life. It turned green with tiny sprouts of grass. Many flowers were blooming everywhere you could see. The huge black castle turned pure white. The sky was clear, and the sun shined on this world after many years for the first time.

"The symbol of good." Venoma saw the palace and thought of what her friend Oliver had said. Right now, he is the only one missing. They landed on the ground smoothly. There were flowers growing all around them on the garden-like area they were standing on. There were four paths from each direction, each leading to the middle of the lovely garden. Four jasmine flower bushes were arranged in a circle. The paths were not blocked by the plants. At the intersection of these pathways stood a structure like a Greek column, and atop it rested the device that links the world of elements and humanity—the box, the first problem they faced.

"Thank you." A soft, kind voice spoke up from behind. The siblings turned to confront a huge crowd. Everyone cheered and clapped, including the men, women, and kids. A few of them were applauding and yelling at them. Some were crying and hugging their kids. Two figures who seemed to be the world's king and queen stood in front of them all.

"Thank you." The Queen said it again. She represented royalty with a tiara perched atop her head. Her golden hair, worn loose, enhanced her already stunning appearance.

"There is no way of how we will be able to express our gratitude." The King said in the same tone as his Queen. It appears as though he also had leaped out of the fairytales. The ideal King, whom everyone must have imagined in their youth.

"It is our honor to be standing here in front of you." Veronica replied when her other two sisters are busy in their own world inside their mind.

"How do we get out of here?" Venoma said immediately. Her elder sister sighed. She must teach her sibling some manners. But the royal couples did not take it seriously. The Queen laughed.

"I understand. You obviously want to return home. Still, I'll present you with two choices. You can retain your abilities and take the place of the previous elemental masters if you remain here. The abilities will disappear and return to the sacred gemstone if you wish to return home. You will gain access to Vigos if you use these stones which will be alongside you. The memories will stay intact."

"We choose option two." The three siblings said without a second thought. But Venoma remembered a horrible fact.

"What happened to Oliver then?" she asked.

"Open that box." The King replied to her question. Veronica did as she was told. Inside only a single stone was there. It was ice blue.

"Your friend was chosen by the master of ice. Every time a manipulator of elements dies, their powers turn into this sacred stone which will patiently wait for its next master." The Queen said gently.

"When we reach home, this dress will also disappear right?" Vespera spoke after a long time.

"What dress..." Veronica and the other sister looked down. Sure enough, it was completely different one from the dress they were wearing before during the battles with the mythical creatures. It looked like a warrior's or...

"This was the same, the group of people were wearing in our memory." Venoma realized. The long cape flowed lightly from the wind. It was of assorted colors too. The colors represent their elements. Red, fire for Veronica, Blue, water for Venoma, and white, wind for Vespera.

"You will go back to the human realm if you wish for it and catch this gemstone of ice." The Queen said pointing to the box.

"Come on." Veronica said to her siblings and...

They were finally going home.

The End...?

"I am bored." Venoma said yet again.

"Some things never change." Veronica said from her desk.

"Trust me, they absolutely don't." Glancing up from her sketchbook, Vespera replied. After their return from Vigos, her drawing skills have reached new heights. When they were gone, time appeared to have stopped. Venoma had opened the box for the first time at midnight. They returned from their terrifying journey at midnight. Just two weeks have passed since that incident, and Venoma's complaints are already back to square one.

"I am bored."

"Say that once more and I am killing you." Veronica reached her limit eventually.

"Calm down fire master. You do not want mess with water." Venoma replied slyly from the center of the room.

"I double dare you to repeat that." The oldest sister said, closing her favorite book.

"You do not want to mess with..." The middle child took the challenge. She ducked to avoid getting beaten up by her older sister, who dashed forward. Venoma climbed on the bed and Veronica obviously chased after her. Venoma seized the opportunity and hit her sister with a pillow. Veronica did the same immediately, laughing.

"Do you mind? I am busy here." Vespera said seriously to her siblings, but her older sisters looked at each other with a smile.

"Oh, you are busy huh?" Venoma attempted to hit her younger sister, but she counterattacked by defending herself. Their eldest sibling also joined the battle. Their room was filled with laughter and joy. It seemed to be the perfect end, right? Wrong.

"What is that?" Venoma said suddenly.

"Oh, for the goodness' sake..." The oldest looked towards the table in disbelief. She was right. The sacred box which was inside her drawer was illuminating light again. Vespera took it out and opened it without wishing she would go back to Vigos. Instead of the four stones, the King's face lit up.

"What's happened?" Veronica asked coming into the view.

"When you were at Vigos... you killed all the enemies right?" The King questioned.

"Is anything wrong?" Vespera asked worried.

"Vigos has transformed to its previous self."

The siblings gasped and looked at each other, not sure if they were dreaming or this is truly the reality. *How did this happen?* "In a few minutes, I will also fade away like the Queen and people. That's why I need your help." The King continued.

"But what could be the reason?" Venoma asked confused.

"Did you kill *Lucifer? The prince of darkness?"*

"Lucifer? “The three siblings asked.

In Vigos, Lucifer looked up at the sky and laughed. He said in the coldest, darkest voice possible

"The Real Fight Begins Now."